"I don't know that it's any of your business!"
said Sticky-toes. FRONTISPIECE. *See page 39.*

The Adventures of Mr. Mocker

THORNTON W. BURGESS

Illustrated by Harrison Cady

PUBLISHED IN ASSOCIATION WITH THE
THORNTON W. BURGESS SOCIETY,
SANDWICH, MASSACHUSETTS
BY
DOVER PUBLICATIONS
GARDEN CITY, NEW YORK

DOVER CHILDREN'S THRIFT CLASSICS
EDITOR OF THIS VOLUME: JANET BAINE KOPITO

Bibliographical Note

This Dover edition, first published by Dover Publications, Inc., in 2011 in association with the Thornton Burgess Society, Sandwich, Massachusetts, who have provided a new Introduction, is an unabridged republication of the work originally published by Little, Brown, and Company, Boston, in 1914.

Library of Congress Cataloging-in-Publication Data

Burgess, Thornton W. (Thornton Waldo), 1874–1965.
  The adventures of Mr. Mocker / Thornton W. Burgess ; illustrated by Harrison Cady. — Dover ed.
    p. cm. — (Dover children's thrift classics)
  Summary: The residents of Green Forest are puzzled by strange sounds, such as Sticky-toes the Tree Toad hearing his own voice coming from another tree, or Sammy Jay keeping everyone awake by calling "Thief, thief!" when he, himself, was asleep.
  ISBN-13: 978-0-486-48101-2
  ISBN-10: 0-486-48101-8
  [1. Tricks—Fiction. 2. Mockingbirds—Fiction. 3. Birds—Fiction. 4. Animals—Fiction.] I. Cady, Harrison, 1877-1970 II. Title.

PZ7. B917Adb 2011
[E]—dc22

2011004993

Manufactured in the United States of America
48101808   2021
www.doverpublications.com

Introduction to the Dover Edition

Thornton Burgess loved birds, and this was evident in his work as a naturalist. Those who consider this Sandwich, Massachusetts, native as just a children's writer are uninformed about the scope of his influence. Although he had only a high school degree, Burgess worked hard to acquire scientific knowledge. Ultimately, he became close friends with many of the most prestigious naturalists of his day, such as Bowdoin College Professor Dr. Alfred Gross and Dr. William Hornaday, Director of the New York Zoological Society and the New York Zoological Park.

Burgess joined with Dr. Hornaday to promote legislation to protect migrating birds, for he feared indiscriminate hunting would lead to the extinction of many avian species. His stories, and a later book, *The Adventures of Poor Mrs. Quack,* highlighted this danger. Although the cause was unpopular with many sportsmen, Burgess and Hornaday were successful in their efforts, which, along with the help of other naturalists, resulted in the passage of the Migratory Bird Treaty Act (1918) by the U.S. Congress.

A short time later, in 1919, Burgess published his *Burgess Bird Book for Children.* It was the first of a series of special children's reference books that dealt with subjects such as birds, animals, flowers, and seashore life. Several naturalists of the day called the work "by far the best bird book for children that we have ever seen."

In 1927, Burgess began a series of serious studies of birds with Dr. Gross. That year they traveled to Panama to view bird life under the auspices of the National Research Council of Washington, D.C. A year later Burgess joined his Bowdoin College friend, Dr. Gross, in what would be an annual expedition to study the last Pinnated Grouse, or Heath Hen, on Martha's Vineyard. This effort ended in 1931, when the hens became extinct. Also in 1931, Burgess and Dr. Gross journeyed to Labrador to study bird life in the Arctic, a trip the author vividly describes in his autobiography, *Now I Remember.*

The Adventures of Mr. Mocker, the mocking bird, was actually the first of Thornton Burgess's many books about birds. In it, the Green Forest folk try to discover who is making noises each night along the Laughing Brook. Mr. Mocker first appeared in a series of bedtime stories written by Burgess for the Associated Newspaper syndicate from October to November of 1912. These stories were collected in book form in 1914. *The Adventures of Mr. Mocker* was republished in Great Britain in 1938. It was also printed in French in Canada in 1948 and translated into Japanese in 1972.

Gene Schott
Director
The Thornton W. Burgess Society
Sandwich, Massachusetts

Contents

List of Illustrations

I
The Lone Traveler

WHEN Mistress Spring starts from way down South to bring joy and gladness to the Green Meadows and the Green Forest, the Laughing Brook and the Smiling Pool, a great many travelers start with her or follow her. Winsome Bluebird goes just a little way ahead of her, for Winsome is the herald of Mistress Spring. Then comes Honker the Goose, and all the world hearing his voice from way, way up in the blue, blue sky knows that truly Mistress Spring is on her way. And with her come Little Friend the Song Sparrow, and Cheerful Robin and Mr. and Mrs. Redwing. Then follow other travelers, ever so many of them, all eager to get back to the beautiful Green Forest and Green Meadows.

Now there are a few feathered folk who think the far away South is quite good enough for them to live there all the year round. Ol' Mistah Buzzard used to think that way. Indeed, he used to think that there was no place like the dear "Ol' Souf," and it wasn't until he went looking for his old friend, Unc' Billy Possum, who had come up to live in the Green Forest, that he found out how nice it is where the Laughing Brook dances down through the Green Forest to the Smiling Pool and then through the Green

1

Meadows to the Big River. Now, when he is sure that there is no danger that he will have cold feet or that he will catch cold in his bald head, he likes to come up to spend the summer near Unc' Billy Possum.

Of course Ol' Mistah Buzzard has wonderful stories to tell when he goes back South in the fall, and all winter long he warms his toes on the chimney tops while he tells his friends about the wonderful things he has seen in his travels. Now there is a certain friend of his, and of Unc' Billy Possum, who had listened to these stories for a long time without seeming in the least interested. But he was. Yes, Sir, he was. He was so much interested that he began to wish he could see for himself all these things Ol' Mistah Buzzard was telling about. But he didn't say a word, not a word. He just listened and listened and then went on about his business.

But when all the other little people in feathers had flown to that far away country Ol' Mistah Buzzard had told about, even Ol' Mistah Buzzard himself, then did this friend of his, and of Unc' Billy Possum, make up his mind that he would go too. He didn't say anything about it to any one, but he just started off by himself. Now of course he didn't know the way, never having been that way before, but he kept on going and going, keeping out of sight as much as he could, and asking no questions. Sometimes he wondered if he would know the Green Forest when he reached it, and then he would remember how

Ol' Mistah Buzzard dearly loves to fly round and round high up in the blue, blue sky.

"All Ah done got to do is to keep on going till Ah see Brer Buzzard," thought he. So he traveled and traveled without speaking to any one, and always looking up in the blue, blue sky. Then one day he saw a black speck high up in the blue, blue sky, and it went round and round and round and round. Finally it dropped down, down, down until it disappeared among the trees.

"It's Brer Buzzard and that must be the Green Forest where Unc' Billy Possum lives," thought the lone traveler, and chuckled. "Ah reckon Ah'll give Unc' Billy a surprise. Yes, Sah, Ah reckon so."

And all the time Unc' Billy Possum and Ol' Mistah Buzzard knew nothing at all about the coming of their old friend and neighbor, but thought him far, far away down in Ol' Virginny where they had left him.

II
Unc' Billy Possum Grows Excited

UNC' BILLY POSSUM sat at the foot of the great hollow tree in which his home is. Unc' Billy felt very fine that morning. He had had a good breakfast, and you know a good breakfast is one of the best things in the world to make one feel fine. Then Unc' Billy's worries were at an end, for Farmer Brown's boy no longer hunted with his dreadful gun through the Green Forest or on the Green Meadows. Then, too, old Granny Fox and Reddy Fox had moved way, way off to the Old Pasture on the edge of the mountain, and so Unc' Billy felt that his eight little Possums could play about without danger.

So he sat with his back to the great hollow tree, wondering if it wouldn't be perfectly safe for him to slip up to Farmer Brown's hen-house in the dark of the next night for some fresh eggs. He could hear old Mrs. Possum cleaning house and scolding the little Possums who kept climbing up on her back. As he listened, Unc' Billy grinned and began to sing in a queer cracked voice:

> "Mah ol' woman am a plain ol' dame—
> 'Deed she am! 'Deed she am!

4

Quick with her broom, with her tongue the same—
    'Deed she am! 'Deed she am!
But she keeps mah house all spick and span;
She has good vittles fo' her ol' man;
She spanks the chillun, but she loves 'em, too;
She sho' am sharp, but she's good and true—
    'Deed she am! 'Deed she am!"

"You'all better stop lazing and hustle about fo' something fo' dinner," said old Mrs. Possum, sticking her sharp little face out of the doorway.

"Yas'm, yas'm, Ah was just aiming to do that very thing," replied Unc' Billy meekly, as he scrambled to his feet.

Just then out tumbled his eight children, making such a racket that Unc' Billy clapped both hands over his ears. "Mah goodness gracious sakes alive!" he exclaimed. One pulled Unc' Billy's tail. Two scrambled up on his back. In two minutes Unc' Billy was down on the ground, rolling and tumbling in the maddest kind of a frolic with his eight children.

Right in the midst of it Unc' Billy sprang to his feet. His eyes were shining, and his funny little ears were pricked up. "Hush, yo'alls!" he commanded. "How do yo'alls think Ah can hear anything with yo'alls making such a racket?" He boxed the ears of one and shook another, and then, when all were still, he stood with his right hand behind his right ear, listening and listening.

"Ah cert'nly thought Ah heard the voice of an ol' friend from way down Souf! Ah cert'nly did!" he muttered, and without another word he started off into the Green Forest, more excited than he had been since his family came up from "Ol' Virginny."

III
Unc' Billy's Vain Search

UNC' BILLY POSSUM was excited. Any one would have known it just to look at him. He hurried off up the Lone Little Path through the Green Forest without even saying good-by to old Mrs. Possum and all the little Possums. They just stared after Unc' Billy and didn't know what to make of it, for such a thing as Unc' Billy forgetting to say good-by had never happened before. Yes, indeed, Unc' Billy certainly was excited.

Old Mrs. Possum sat in the doorway of their home in the great hollow tree and watched Unc' Billy out of sight. Her sharp little eyes seemed to grow sharper as she watched. "Ah done sent that no-account Possum to hunt fo' something fo' dinner, but 'pears to me he's plumb forgot it already," she muttered. "Just look at him with his head up in the air like he thought dinner fo' we uns would drap right down to him out o' the sky! If he's aiming to find a bird's nest with eggs in it this time o' year, he sho'ly am plumb foolish in his haid. No, Sah! That onery Possum has clean fo'gotten what Ah just done tole him, and if we uns am going to have any dinner, Ah cert'nly have got to flax 'round right smart spry mahself!"

Such a thing as Unc' Billy forgetting to say good-by
had never happened before. *Page 7*.

Old Mrs. Possum chased the eight little Possums into the house and warned them not to so much as put their heads outside the door while she was gone. Then she started out to hunt for their dinner, still muttering as she went.

Old Mrs. Possum was quite right. Unc' Billy had forgotten all about that dinner. You see he had something else on his mind. While he had been playing with his children, he had thought that he heard a voice way off in the distance, and it had sounded very, very much like the voice of an old friend from way down South in "Ol' Virginny." He had listened and listened but didn't hear it again, and yet he was sure he had heard it that once. The very thought that that old friend of his might be somewhere in the Green Forest excited Unc' Billy so that it fairly made him homesick. He just *had* to go look for him.

So all the rest of that day Unc' Billy Possum walked and walked through the Green Forest, peering up in the tree-tops and looking into the bushes until his neck ached. But nowhere did he catch a glimpse of his old friend. The longer he looked, the more excited he grew.

"What's the matter with you?" asked Jimmy Skunk, meeting Unc' Billy on the Crooked Little Path near the top of the hill.

"Nuffin, nuffin, Sah! Ah'm just walking fo' mah health," replied Unc' Billy over his shoulder, as he hurried on. You see he didn't like to tell any one what he thought he had heard, for fear that it might not be true, and then they would laugh at him.

"Didn't suppose Unc' Billy ever worried about his health," muttered Jimmy Skunk with a puzzled look, as he watched Unc' Billy disappear.

Just as jolly, round, red Mr. Sun dropped out of sight behind the Purple Hills, Unc' Billy gave it up and turned toward home. His neck ached from looking up in the tree-tops, and his feet were sore from walking. And just then Unc' Billy for the first time thought of that dinner that old Mrs. Possum had sent him to get. Unc' Billy sat down and mopped his brow in dismay.

"Ah 'specks Ah'm in fo' it this time, sho' enough!" he said.

IV
Unc' Billy Comes Home

UNC' BILLY POSSUM crept along in the darkest shadows he could find as he drew near to the great hollow tree which is his home.

"Ah 'specks Ah'm in fo' it. Ah 'specks Ah sho'ly am in fo' it this time," he kept muttering.

So Unc' Billy crept along in the black shadows until he got where he could look up and see his own doorway. Then he sat down and watched a while. All was still. There wasn't a sound in the great hollow tree.

"Perhaps mah ol' woman am out calling, and Ah can slip in and go to bed before she gets back," said Unc' Billy hopefully to himself, as he started to climb the great hollow tree.

But at the first scratch of his toe-nails on the bark the sharp face of old Mrs. Possum appeared in the doorway.

"Good evening, mah dear," said Unc' Billy, in the mildest kind of a voice.

Old Mrs. Possum said nothing, but Unc' Billy felt as if her sharp black eyes were looking right through him.

Unc' Billy grinned a sickly kind of grin as he said:

"Ah hopes yo'alls are feeling good tonight."

"Where's that dinner Ah sent yo' fo'?" demanded old Mrs. Possum sharply.

Unc' Billy fidgeted uneasily. "Ah done brought yo' two eggs from Farmer Brown's hen-house," he replied meekly.

"Two eggs! Two eggs! How do yo' think Ah am going to feed eight hungry mouths on two eggs?" snapped old Mrs. Possum.

Unc' Billy hung his head. He hadn't a word to say. He just couldn't tell her that he had spent the whole day tramping through the Green Forest looking for an old friend, whose voice he had thought he heard, when he ought to have been helping her find a dinner for the eight little Possums. No, Sir, Unc' Billy hadn't a word to say.

My, my, my, how old Mrs. Possum did scold, as she came down the great hollow tree to get the two eggs. Unc' Billy knew that he deserved every bit of it. He felt very miserable, and he was too tired to have a bit of spirit left. So he just sat at the foot of the great hollow tree and said nothing, while old Mrs. Possum bit a hole in the end of one egg and began to suck it. All the time she was looking at Unc' Billy with those sharp eyes of hers. When she had finished the egg, she pushed the other over to him.

"Yo' eat that!" she said shortly. "Yo' look as if yo' hadn't had anything to eat to-day" (which was true). "Then yo' hustle up to bed; it's all ready fo' yo'."

Unc' Billy did as he was bid, and as he tucked himself into his snug, warm bed he murmured sleepily:

"Ol' Mrs. Possum has a sharp, sharp tongue,
But her bark is worse than her bite.
For Ol' Mrs. Possum has a soft, soft heart
Though she hides it way out of sight."

V
Sammy Jay is Indignant

SAMMY JAY was indignant. Yes, Sir, Sammy Jay was very much put out. In fact, Sammy was just plain downright mad! It is bad enough to be found out and blamed for the things you really do, but to be blamed for things that you don't do and don't even know anything about is more than even Mr. Jaybird can stand. It had begun when he met Jimmy Skunk early in the morning.

"Hello, Sammy Jay! What were you doing up so late last night?" said Jimmy Skunk.

"I wasn't up late; I went to bed at my usual hour, just after Mr. Sun went to bed behind the Purple Hills," replied Sammy Jay.

"Oh, come, Sammy Jay, be honest for once in your life! It was a long, long, long time after Mr. Sun went to bed that I heard you screaming and making a great fuss over in the Green Forest. What was it all about?"

Sammy Jay stamped one foot. He was beginning to lose his temper. You know he loses it very easily. "I am honest!" he screamed. "I tell you I went to bed just as I always do, and I didn't wake up until this morning."

"Then you must talk something dreadful in your sleep," said Jimmy Skunk, turning his back on Sammy Jay, who was so mad by this time that for a few minutes he couldn't find his tongue. When he did, he flew off screaming at the top of his lungs. He was still screaming when he flew over the Old Briar-patch where Peter Rabbit was just beginning to doze off.

Peter was sleepy. He didn't like to have his morning nap disturbed.

"Hi, Sammy Jay! Didn't you make racket enough last night to give honest folks a little peace and quiet to-day?" shouted Peter Rabbit.

Sammy Jay flew up into a young cherry tree on the edge of the Old Briar-patch, and his eyes were fairly red with anger as he glared down at Peter Rabbit.

"What's the joke, Peter Rabbit? That's the second time this morning that I've been told that I was screaming last night, when all the time I was fast asleep," said Sammy Jay.

"Then it's a funny way you have of sleeping," replied Peter Rabbit. "Come, Sammy, be honest and tell me what you were yelling 'thief' for, over in the Green Forest?"

"Peter Rabbit, you and Jimmy Skunk are crazy, just as crazy as loons!" sputtered Sammy Jay. "I tell you I was asleep, and I guess I ought to know!"

"And I guess I know your voice when I hear it!" replied Peter Rabbit. "It's bad enough in daytime, but if I was you, I'd quit yelling in the night. Some one of these times Hooty the Owl will hear you, and that will be the end of you and your noise. Now go away; I want to sleep."

Sammy went. He was mad clear through, and yet he didn't know what to make of it. Were they just trying to make him mad, or had he really been screaming in his sleep? He flew over to the Smiling Pool. Jerry Muskrat looked up and saw him.

"What were you yelling about in the night, Sammy Jay?" asked Jerry.

This was too much. Sammy Jay let his wings and his tail droop dejectedly and hung his head.

"I don't know. I really don't know anything about it," he said.

VI
Sammy Jay Thinks He's Going Crazy

"Sammy Jay screams all day long,
    And now what do you think?
Why, Sammy sits and yells all night
    And doesn't sleep a wink!"

EVERYWHERE he went Sammy Jay heard that shouted after him. Dozens and dozens of times a day he heard it. At first he lost his temper and was the very maddest Jaybird ever seen on the Green Meadows or in the Green Forest.

"It isn't true! It isn't true! It isn't true!" he would scream at the top of his lungs.

And then everybody within hearing would shout: "It *is* true!"

Sammy would just dance up and down and scream and scream and scream, he was so angry. And then he was sure to hear some one pipe up:

"Sammy's mad and we are glad,
    And we know how to tease him!
But some dark night he'll get a fright,
    For Hooty'll come and seize him!"

That really began to worry him. At first he had thought that it was all a joke on the part of the little

17

people of the Green Forest and the Green Meadows, and that they had made up the story about hearing him in the night. Then he began to think that it might be true that he did talk in his sleep, and this worried him a whole lot. If he did that, Hooty the Owl would surely find him sooner or later, and in the morning there wouldn't be anything left of him but a few feathers from his fine coat.

The more he thought about it, the more worried Sammy Jay became. He lost his appetite and began to grow thin. He kept out of sight whenever possible and no longer screamed "Thief! thief!" through the Green Forest. In fact his voice was rarely heard during the day. But it seemed that he must be talking just as much as ever in the night. At least everybody said that he was. Worse still, different ones said that they heard him in different places in the Green Forest and even down on the Green Meadows. Could it be that he was flying about as well as talking in his sleep? And nobody believed him when he said that he was asleep all night. They thought that he was awake and doing it purposely. They might have known that he couldn't see in the night, for his eyes are made for daylight and not for darkness, like the eyes of Boomer the Nighthawk and Hooty the Owl. But they didn't seem to think of this, and insisted that almost every night they heard him down in the alders along the Laughing Brook. Yet every morning when he awoke, Sammy would find himself just where he went to sleep the night before, safely hidden in the thickest part of a big pine-tree.

"If they are not all crazy, then I must be," said Sammy Jay to himself, as he turned away from the breakfast which he could not eat. Then he had a happy idea. "Why didn't I think of it before? I'll sleep all day, and then I'll keep awake all night and see what happens then!" he exclaimed.

So Sammy Jay hurried away to the darkest part of the Green Forest and tried to sleep through the day.

VII
Sammy Jay Sits up all Night

SAMMY JAY sat in the dark and shivered. Sammy was lonely, more lonely than he had ever supposed anybody could be. And to tell the truth Sammy Jay was scared. Yes, Sir, that was just the way Sammy Jay felt—scared. Every time a leaf rustled, Sammy jumped almost out of his skin. His heart went pit-a-pat, pit-a-pat, pit-a-pat. He could hear it himself, or at least he thought he could, and it seemed to him that if Hooty the Owl should happen to come along, he would surely hear it.

You see it was the first time in all his life that Sammy Jay had not gone to sleep just as soon as jolly, round, red Mr. Sun had pulled his rosy nightcap on and gone to bed behind the Purple Hills. But to-night Sammy sat in the darkest, thickest part of a big pine-tree and kept blinking his eyes to keep from going to sleep. He had made up his mind that he wouldn't go to sleep at all that night, no matter how lonely and frightened he might be. He just would keep his eyes and his ears wide open.

What was he doing it for? Why, because all the little meadow and forest people insisted that every night lately Sammy Jay had spent a great part of his time screaming in the harsh, unpleasant way he does during the day, and some of them were very cross, because they said that he waked them up when they wanted to sleep. Now Sammy knew better. He never in his life had screamed in the night unless—well, unless he did it in his sleep and didn't know it. So he had made up his mind to keep awake all of this night and see if in the morning any one would say that he had waked them up.

He had watched the black shadows creep through the Green Forest and grow blacker and blacker. The blacker they grew, the lonesomer he became. By and by it was so dark that he couldn't see anything at all, and every little noise made him shiver. It is easy to be brave in daylight, but in the dark, when you cannot see a thing, every little sound seems twice as loud as it really is and gives you such a creepy, creepy feeling. Sammy Jay had it now. He felt so creepy that it seemed as if he would crawl right out of his skin. He kept saying over and over to himself: "There's nothing to be afraid of. There's nothing to be afraid of. I'm just as safe as if I was fast asleep." But still he shivered and shook.

By and by, looking up through the top of the big pine-tree, he saw the little stars come out one by one. They seemed to be looking right down at him and winking at him in the jolliest way. Somehow, he didn't feel quite so lonely then, and he tried to wink back. Then little, soft, silvery bars of light began to creep through the branches of the trees and along the ground. They were moonbeams, and Sammy could see just a little, a very little. He began to feel better.

"Whooo-hoo-hoo, whooo-hoo!"

It was a terrible sound, fierce and hungry. Sammy Jay nearly fell from his perch. He opened his mouth to scream with fright. Then he remembered just in time and closed it without a sound. It was the hunting-cry of Hooty the Owl. Sammy Jay sat huddled in a little, forlorn, shivering heap, while twice more that fierce cry rang through the Green Forest. Then a shadow floated over the big pine-tree. Hooty the Owl had flown away without seeing him, and Sammy breathed easier.

VIII
Sammy Jay is Glad He Sat up all Night

SAMMY JAY was having no trouble in keeping awake now. Not a bit! He couldn't have gone to sleep if he wanted to—not since Hooty the Owl had frightened him almost out of his skin with his fierce, hungry hunting-call. He was too frightened and shivery and creepy to sleep. But he didn't want to, anyway.

So he sat in the thickest part of the big pine-tree, shivering and creepy and miserable. He heard Bobby Coon go down the Lone Little Path on his way to Farmer Brown's cornfield, where the corn was just beginning to get milky and sweet. Out in a patch of bright moonlight he saw Peter Rabbit jumping and dancing and having the greatest kind of a time all by himself. Pretty soon Peter was joined by his cousin, Jumper the Hare. Such antics as they did cut up! Sammy Jay almost laughed aloud as he watched. It was less lonely with them there, and he did want to call to them dreadfully. But that would never, never do, for no one must know that he was sitting up awake all night.

By and by along came Jimmy Skunk, walking out into the patch of bright moonlight. He touched noses with Peter Rabbit and Jumper the Hare, which is one way of saying "good evening" in the Green Forest.

"Isn't it most time for Sammy Jay to scream in his sleep?" asked Peter Rabbit.

Sammy pricked up his ears. "Scream in his sleep! Nonsense! Sammy Jay isn't any more asleep than I am. He just screams out of pure meanness to wake up and frighten good honest folks who want to sleep. For my part, I don't see what any one wants to sleep for on such a fine night as this, anyway. It serves 'em right if they do get waked up," replied Jimmy Skunk.

"But Sammy Jay says that he doesn't do it and doesn't know anything about it," said Peter Rabbit. "Have you ever seen him scream in the night, Jimmy Skunk?"

"No, I don't have to," replied Jimmy Skunk. "I guess I know his voice when I hear it, and I've heard it enough times the last few nights, goodness knows! Tell me this, Peter Rabbit: who else is there that cries 'Thief! thief! thief!' and screams like Sammy Jay?"

Peter shook his head. "I guess you're right, Jimmy Skunk. I guess you're right," he said.

"Of course I'm right. There, now!" Jimmy held up one hand to warn Peter to keep still. Sure enough, there was Sammy Jay's voice, way over in the alders beside the Laughing Brook, and it was screaming "Thief! thief! thief!"

They all heard it. Sammy Jay heard it, too, and scratched himself to be sure that he was awake and sitting there in the big pine-tree.

"It's my voice, and it isn't my voice, for I haven't made a sound, and it's over in the alders while I'm here in my own big pine-tree," muttered Sammy Jay to himself. "I'm glad I kept awake, but—

"Maybe I'm going crazy!
My wits are getting hazy!
That's surely me,
Yet here I be!
Oh, dear, I sure am crazy!"

IX
The Mystery Grows

"Can a body be a body,
    Yet not a body be?
Tell a body, anybody,
    Didst such a body see?"

OF course it was Sammy Jay who was humming such a foolish-sounding rhyme as that. But really, it wasn't so foolish in Sammy's case, after all. He had sat up wide awake all night just to try to find out why it was that all the little meadow and forest people had complained that he spent part of each night screaming "Thief! thief! thief!" just as he does in the daytime. Now he knew. Sitting in the dark in his big pine-tree, he had heard his own voice, or what sounded like his own voice, screaming down in the alders by the Laughing Brook. Sammy had scratched himself to be sure that he was really and truly awake and not dreaming, for there was his voice down in the alders, and there was himself sitting in the big pine tree with his mouth closed as tight as he could shut it. Did ever a Jaybird have anything so queer as that to puzzle him?

Anyway, Sammy Jay knew that he didn't scream in his sleep, and there was a whole lot of comfort in that. He could eat with a better appetite now. You see, when he had been told that he was screaming in the night, Sammy had been afraid that he was doing it in his sleep; and if he was doing that, why, some dark night Hooty the Owl might hear him and find him, and that would be the end of him. Now he knew that he could go to sleep in peace, just as he always had.

Sammy Jay brushed and smoothed out his handsome blue coat and made himself as pert and smart-appearing as possible. He had been so worried lately that he hadn't taken much care of himself, which is very unusual for Sammy Jay. Now, however, he felt so much better that he began to think about his looks. When he had finished dressing, he started for the alders beside the Laughing Brook just to have a look around. Of course he didn't expect to find his voice down there, for who ever saw a voice? Still he thought that he might find something that would explain the mystery.

He hunted all around in the thicket of alders beside the Laughing Brook, but nothing unusual did he find. Then for a long time he sat as still as still can be, studying and thinking. Finally he thought to himself: "I'll just see how my voice really does sound down here," and opening his mouth he screamed:

"Thief! thief! thief!"

Then out popped Jenny Wren, and she was so mad that she couldn't sit still a second. My, my, my, how she did scold!

"You ought to be ashamed of yourself, Sammy Jay! You ought to be ashamed of yourself!" she sputtered. "Isn't it enough to keep us awake half the night without coming down and screaming all day?"

"I haven't been down here in the night, and I haven't kept anybody awake!" replied Sammy Jay indignantly.

Jenny Wren came right up in front of Sammy Jay and hopped up and down. She was so mad that with every word she jerked her funny little tail so that Sammy Jay almost had to laugh.

"Don't tell that to me, Sammy Jay! Don't tell that to me!" she cried. "Didn't I see you with my own eyes sitting in that alder over there? Don't tell that to me! You ought to be ashamed of yourself!"

X
Sammy Jay Seeks Advice

SAMMY JAY had a headache, such a headache! He had thought and thought and thought, until now it seemed to him that the world surely had turned topsy-turvy. His poor little head was all in a whirl, and that was what made it ache. First he had been accused of screaming in the night to waken and scare the little meadow and forest people who wanted to sleep. Then he had kept awake all night to find out what it meant, and he had heard what sounded like his own voice screaming "Thief! thief! thief!" down by the Laughing Brook, when all the time he was sitting in the dark in his own big pine-tree in the Green Forest.

That was bad enough, but to have Jenny Wren tell him that she had seen him with her own eyes sitting in an alder tree and screaming, at the very time that he had been back there in the big pine-tree, was more than Sammy Jay could stand. It was no wonder that his head ached. Hardly any of the little meadow and forest people would speak to him now. They just turned their backs to him whenever he met them. He didn't mind this so much, because he knew that none of them had ever liked him very well. You see he had played too many mean tricks for any one to really like him. But he did hate to have them blame him for something that he hadn't done.

"It's too much for me!" said Sammy Jay. "It's too much for me! I've thought and thought, until my brain just goes round and round and makes me dizzy, and my thoughts turn somersaults over each other. I must get help somewhere. Now, who can I go to, so few will have anything to do with me?"

"Caw, caw, caw!"

Sammy Jay pricked up his ears and spread his wings. "My cousin, Blacky the Crow!" he cried. "Why didn't I think of him before? He's very smart, is Blacky the Crow, and perhaps he can tell me what to do."

So Sammy Jay hurried as fast as he could to lay his troubles before Blacky the Crow. Blacky's eyes twinkled as he listened to Sammy Jay's tale of woe. When Sammy had finished and had asked for Blacky's advice, Blacky went into a black study. Sammy sat and waited patiently, for he felt certain that Blacky's shrewd head would find some plan to solve the mystery.

"I don't know how you can find out who it is that's making you all this trouble, but I'll tell you how you can prove that it isn't you that screams in the night," said Blacky the Crow after a while.

"How?" asked Sammy Jay eagerly.

"Go away from the Green Meadows and the Green Forest and stay away for a week," replied Blacky the Crow. "Go up to the far-away Old Pasture on the

Blacky's eyes twinkled as he listened to
Sammy Jay's tale of woe. *Page 30.*

edge of the mountain, where Reddy and Granny Fox are living. Have Boomer the Nighthawk see you go to bed there, and then ask him to come straight down here and tell Peter Rabbit just where you are. Peter will tell every one else, for he can't keep his tongue still, and then they'll all know that it isn't you that screams in the night."

"The very thing!" cried Sammy Jay. "I'll move at once!" And off he hurried to prepare to move up to the Old Pasture.

XI
How Blacky the Crow's Plan Worked Out

"THIEF! thief! thief!" Old Granny Fox, trotting along a cow-path in the Old Pasture on the edge of the mountain, heard it and grinned. Reddy Fox, sitting in the doorway of their new home under the great rocks in the midst of the thickest clump of bushes and young trees, heard it, too, and he grinned even more broadly than Granny Fox. It sounded good to him, did that harsh scream, for it was the first time he had heard the voice of a single one of the little meadow and forest people since he and Granny Fox had moved up to the lonesome Old Pasture.

"Now I wonder what has brought Sammy Jay way up here?" said Reddy, as he limped out to the edge of the thick tangle of bushes and young trees. Pretty soon he caught sight of a wonderful coat of bright blue with white trimmings.

"Hi, Sammy Jay! What are you doing up here?" shouted Reddy Fox.

Sammy Jay heard him and hurried over to where Reddy Fox was sitting.

"Hello, Reddy Fox! How are you feeling?" said Sammy Jay.

"Better, thank you. What are you doing way up here in this lonely place?" replied Reddy.

33

"It's a long story," said Sammy Jay.

"Tell it to me," begged Reddy Fox.

So Sammy Jay told him all about the trouble he had had on the Green Meadows and in the Green Forest, and how hardly any one would speak to him because they said that he kept them awake by screaming in the night. He told how he had sat up all night and had heard what sounded like his own voice, when all the time he was sitting with his mouth shut as tight as tight could be. Then he told about Blacky the Crow's plan, which was that Sammy should come to the Old Pasture and live for a week. Then, if the little people of the Green Meadows and the Green Forest heard screams in the night, they would know that it was not Sammy Jay who was waking them up. Reddy Fox chuckled as he listened. You know misery likes company, and it tickled Reddy to think that some one else had been forced to leave the Green Meadows and the Green Forest.

That night Sammy Jay found a comfortable place which seemed quite safe in which to go to sleep. Just after jolly, round, red Mr. Sun went to bed behind the Purple Hills, Sammy saw Boomer the Nighthawk circling round high in the air catching his dinner. Sammy screamed twice. Boomer heard him and down he came with a rush.

"Why, Sammy Jay, what under the sun are you doing way off here?" exclaimed Boomer.

"Going to bed," replied Sammy. "Say, Boomer, will you do something for me?"

"That depends upon what it is," replied Boomer.

"It's just an errand," replied Sammy Jay, and then he asked Boomer to go down to the Green Meadows and tell Peter Rabbit how he, Boomer, had seen Sammy going to bed up in the far-away Old Pasture.

Boomer promised that he would, and off he started. He found Peter and told him. Of course Peter was very much surprised and, because he cannot keep his tongue still, he started off at once to tell everybody he could find, just as Blacky the Crow had thought he would do.

XII
No One Believes Peter Rabbit

PETER RABBIT sat in his secret place in the middle of the Old Briar-patch. Peter was doing some very hard thinking. He ought to have been asleep, for he had been out the whole night long. But instead of sleeping, he was wide awake and thinking and thinking.

You see early the night before Boomer the Nighthawk had told Peter that Sammy Jay was up in the far-away Old Pasture. Boomer had seen him going to bed there and had come straight down to tell Peter. This was great news, and Peter could hardly wait for Boomer to stop talking, he was so anxious to spread the news over the Green Meadows and through the Green Forest, for Peter is a great gossip and cannot keep his tongue still.

So he had hurried this way and that way, telling every one he met how Sammy Jay had moved away to the Old Pasture. But no one believed him.

"Wait and see! Wait and see!" said Jimmy Skunk.

"It's just a trick," said Bobby Coon.

"But Boomer the Nighthawk saw him up there going to bed and talked with him!" cried Peter Rabbit.

"Perhaps he did and then again perhaps he didn't," replied Bobby Coon, carefully washing an ear of sweet milky corn that he had brought down to the Laughing Brook from Farmer Brown's corn-field, for Bobby Coon is very, very neat and always washes his food before eating. "For my part," he continued, "I believe that Boomer the Nighthawk just made up that story to help Sammy Jay fool us."

"But that would be a wrong story, and I don't believe that Boomer would do anything like that!" cried Peter.

Just then there was a shrill scream of "Thief! thief! thief!" over in the alder bushes. It certainly sounded like Sammy Jay's voice.

"What did I tell you? Now what do you think?" cried Bobby Coon.

Peter didn't know what to think, and he said so. He left Bobby to eat his corn and spent the rest of the night telling every one he met what Boomer the Nighthawk had said, but of course no one believed it, and every one laughed at him, for hadn't they heard Sammy Jay screaming that very night?

So now Peter sat in the Old Briar-patch thinking and thinking, when he should have been asleep. Finally he yawned and stretched and then started along one of his private little paths.

"I'll just run up to the Green Forest and try to find Sammy Jay," he said.

So Peter hunted and hunted all through the Green Forest for Sammy Jay, and asked everybody he met if they had seen Sammy. But no one had, though every one took pains to tell Peter that they had heard

Sammy in the night. At last Peter found Sticky-toes the Tree Toad. He was muttering and grumbling to himself, and he didn't see Peter. Peter stopped to listen, which was, of course, a very wrong thing to do, and what he heard gave Peter an idea.

XIII
Sticky-Toes the Tree Toad
Pours out His Troubles

STICKY-TOES was quite upset. There was no doubt about it. Either he had gotten out of the wrong side of his bed that morning, or his breakfast had disagreed with him, or something had happened to make him lose his temper completely.

"Don't know what it means! Don't know what it means! Don't know what it means!" croaked Sticky-toes the Tree Toad, over and over again. "Heard it last night and the night before that and before that and before that and before that, and I don't know what it means!"

"Don't know what what means?" asked Peter Rabbit, whose curiosity would not let him keep still.

"Hello, Long-ears! I don't know that it's any of your business!" said Sticky-toes.

Peter allowed that it wasn't, but that as he had so much on his own mind he couldn't help being interested when he found that Sticky-toes had troubles too. Then he told Sticky-toes all about how Boomer the Nighthawk had said that he had seen Sammy Jay going to bed up in the far-away Old Pasture, and how that very night Sammy Jay's voice had been heard screaming down in the alders beside the Laughing Brook. Sticky-toes nodded his head.

"I heard it," said he.

"But how could Sammy Jay be down here if he went to bed way off there in the Old Pasture? Tell me that, Sticky-toes?" said Peter Rabbit.

Sticky-toes shook his head. "Don't ask me! Don't ask me! Just tell me how it is that I hear my own voice when I don't speak a word," said Sticky-toes the Tree Toad.

"What's that?" exclaimed Peter Rabbit.

Then Sticky-toes poured out all his troubles to Peter Rabbit. They were very much like the troubles of Sammy Jay. Every night Sticky-toes would hear what sounded like his own voice coming from a tree in which he was not sitting at all, and at a time when he was keeping his mouth shut as tight as he knew how. In fact, he had been so worried that for several nights he hadn't said a word, yet his neighbors had complained that he had been very noisy. He was getting so worried that he couldn't eat.

Peter Rabbit listened with his mouth wide open. It was just the same kind of a story that Sammy Jay had told. What under the sun could be going on? Peter couldn't understand it at all. It certainly was very, very curious. He just must find out about it!

XIV
Peter Rabbit Meets Unc' Billy Possum

AFTER Sticky-toes the Tree Toad had poured out his troubles, Peter went back to the Old Briar-patch, more puzzled than ever. If Sammy Jay was asleep in the far-away Old Pasture on the edge of the mountain, how could he be at the same time down in the Green Forest screaming? And if Sticky-toes the Tree Toad sat all night with his mouth shut tight, how could the voice of Sticky-toes be heard in an altogether different tree than the one Sticky-toes was spending the night in? Wasn't it enough to drive any one crazy?

The more Peter studied over it, the more puzzled he grew. The next night he started out for the Green Forest with a new plan in his head. He would hide down among the alders by the Laughing Brook. He would see for himself who was screaming with the voice of Sammy Jay and talking with the voice of Sticky-toes the Tree Toad. He just had to know!

So across the Green Meadows and up the Lone Little Path hurried Peter Rabbit, so as to reach the Laughing Brook before jolly, round, red Mr. Sun had wholly turned out his light, after going to bed behind the Purple Hills. He was hurrying so that he almost ran into Unc' Billy Possum.

"Yo' seem to be in a powerful hurry, Brer Rabbit," said Unc' Billy.

"I am," replied Peter. "I must get down to the Laughing Brook before dark."

"'Pears to me it must be mighty impo'tant to make yo' hurry this way," said Unc' Billy Possum.

"It is," replied Peter Rabbit. "It's to keep me from going crazy."

Unc' Billy looked at Peter very hard for a few minutes, just as if he thought that Peter was crazy already. Then he put a hand behind one ear just as if he was hard of hearing. "Ah beg yo' pardon, Brer Rabbit, but Ah don' seem to have it quite right in mah haid what yo'all am going down to the Laughing Brook for," said Unc' Billy in the politest way.

Peter chuckled in spite of himself, as he once more replied:

"It's to keep me from going crazy."

"Then Peter told Unc' Billy all about Sammy Jay's troubles and all about the troubles of Sticky-toes the Tree Toad. It was the first Unc' Billy Possum had heard about it, for Unc' Billy had been away from the Green Forest and the Green Meadows for a visit and had just returned. He listened to all that Peter Rabbit had to say, and a funny, pleased sort of look came into his eyes.

"Ah reckon Ah will go along with yo'all," said he.

So Unc' Billy Possum went with Peter Rabbit to the Laughing Brook, where they hid underneath the alders.

XV
Peter Rabbit and Unc' Billy Possum Keep Watch

"NOW," said Peter Rabbit, as they settled themselves to watch, "we'll see for ourselves whether Sammy Jay and Sticky-toes have been telling the truth, or if they have been dreaming. If we hear Sammy Jay's voice down here in the alders tonight, we ought to be able to see who is using it, for pretty soon the moon will be up, and then we can see easily."

Unc' Billy Possum didn't say anything, not a word, but if Peter Rabbit had noticed Unc' Billy's eyes, he would have seen a very knowing look there. The fact is, Unc' Billy was thinking of the time when he thought he had heard the voice of an old friend of his from way down South, and he was beginning to suspect that he had been right, and that his old friend really was somewhere in the Green Forest.

"Ah reckon he sho'ly is, and he's plumb full of his ol' tricks, just like he used to be," muttered Unc' Billy.

"What's that?" asked Peter, pricking up his ears.

"Nothing, nothing, Brer Rabbit, nothing at all. Ah has a habit of just talking foolishness to mahself," replied Unc' Billy.

Peter looked at him sharply, but Unc' Billy's shrewd little face looked so innocent that Peter was ashamed to doubt what Unc' Billy said.

"I guess that we better not talk any more, for fear we might be heard and have our watch for nothing," said Peter.

Unc' Billy agreed, and side by side they sat as still as if they were made of wood or stone. The black shadows came early to the alders beside the Laughing Brook, and soon it was very dark, so dark that Peter and Unc' Billy, whose eyes are meant for seeing in the dark as well as in the light, had hard work to make out much. It grew later and later, and still there was not a sound of the voice of either Sammy Jay or Sticky-toes the Tree Toad. Peter began to get hungry. The more he thought about it, the hungrier he grew. He was just about ready to give it up, when the moonbeams began to creep in among the alder trees just as they had crept through the Green Forest the night that Sammy Jay kept awake all night.

The moonbeams crept farther and farther into the thicket of alder trees and bushes where Peter Rabbit and Unc' Billy Possum were hiding. Then it was that they heard the voice of Sticky-toes the Tree Toad. At any rate, Peter was sure that it was the voice of Sticky-toes until a fierce, angry whisper came down to him from the branch of an alder just over his head. Peter looked up. There sat Sticky-toes himself, but his voice was coming from an alder on the other side of the Laughing Brook.

"Do you hear that? Do you hear that? There's my voice over there, and here I am here! What do you make of it?" whispered Sticky-toes.

Peter didn't know what to make of it. All he could do was to gaze at Sticky-toes as if he thought Sticky-toes was a ghost. Just then the voice of Sammy Jay, or what sounded for all the world like Sammy's voice, screamed "Thief! thief! thief!" from the very spot where they had just heard the voice of Sticky-toes.

Peter turned to ask Unc' Billy Possum what he thought, but Unc' Billy wasn't there.

XVI
Unc' Billy Possum Does a
Little Surprising Himself

WHEN Unc' Billy Possum first heard what sounded like the voice of Sticky-toes the Tree Toad, he had thought, just as Peter Rabbit did, that Sticky-toes was over in an alder tree on the other side of the Laughing Brook. But when he heard a whisper right over their heads and looked up to see Sticky-toes himself, Unc' Billy almost chuckled out loud.

> "Yo' can't fool Uncle Billy,
> So don't go fo' to try!
> Ah knows yo', yes, Ah knows yo'—
> Ah knows yo', Mistah Sly."

He said that to himself and quite under his breath, for all the time that Peter Rabbit and Sticky-toes the Tree Toad were whispering together, Unc' Billy Possum was stealing away under the alder bushes. Unc' Billy is very soft-footed, oh, very soft-footed indeed, when he wants to be. You see one must needs be very soft-footed to steal eggs in Farmer Brown's hen-house. So Unc' Billy stole away without making a sound, and when Peter Rabbit turned to speak to him, there was no Unc' Billy there.

46

Peter rubbed his eyes and stared all around, this way and that way, but no sign of Unc' Billy could he see. This so surprised Peter Rabbit that he felt queer all over. First there was the voice of Sticky-toes over on the other side of the Laughing Brook, when all the time Sticky-toes wasn't there at all. Now here Unc' Billy Possum had disappeared, just as if the earth had swallowed him up.

"This isn't any place for me!" said Peter Rabbit, and off he started for the Green Meadows as fast as he could go, lipperty-lipperty-lip!

All this time Unc' Billy Possum had been crawling along without the tiniest sound. When he came to the Laughing Brook, he went up a way until he found a big tree with a branch stretching clear across. Of course Unc' Billy could have swum across, but he didn't feel like swimming that night, so he climbed up the big tree, ran out along the branch, let himself down by the tail, and then dropped. He was across the Laughing Brook without even wetting his feet.

Unc' Billy didn't waste any time. Just as soft-footed as before, he crept along in the darkest shadows, until he was right under the alder tree from which the complaining voice of Sticky-toes the Tree Toad seemed to come. Unc' Billy listened, and the longer he listened, the broader grew the smile on Unc' Billy's shrewd face.

"Thief! thief! thief!"

It certainly sounded for all the world like Sammy Jay's voice, and it was right over Unc' Billy's head.

Unc' Billy peered up through the alders. The leaves were so thick that he could not see very well, but what he did see was enough. It was a long tail, a tail of feathers hanging down. It wasn't Sammy Jay's tail, either.

"Don' yo'all think that yo'all have joked enough?" asked Unc' Billy, trying hard to keep from chuckling aloud.

A cry of "Thief" stopped right in the middle, and two sharp eyes looked down in surprise at Unc' Billy.

XVII
The Meeting of Two Old Friends

"WHY, Unc' Billy Possum! What are yo'all doing way up here?" cried the owner of the long tail and sharp eyes.

"This is mah home now. Ah done moved up here," replied Unc' Billy. "'Pears to me that the question is what am yo'all doing way off up here? Ah thought Ah sho'ly done hear your voice the other day, and Ah most wore mah po' feet out looking fo' yo'. Ah thought Ah was mistaken, but now Ah reckon that Ah was right, after all. My, but Ah am right smart glad to see yo'!"

"Thank yo', Unc' Billy," replied the owner of the long tail and the sharp eyes. "Ah reckon yo' can't be any more glad to see me, than Ah am to see yo'. Fact is, Ah was getting right smart lonesome. Ah done been lying low daytimes, because, yo' know, Ah'm a stranger up here, and Ah was afraid that strangers might not be welcome in the Green Forest and on the Green Meadows."

"'Pears like if all Ah hear am true, that yo' haven't done much lying low nights. Ah reckon yo' done make up fo' those lonesome feelings. Yes, Sah, Ah reckon so. Mah goodness, man, yo' done set everybody to running around like they was crazy!" exclaimed Unc' Billy.

The owner of the long tail and sharp eyes threw back his head and laughed, and his laugh was like the most beautiful music. It made Unc' Billy feel good just listening to it.

"Sammy Jay done moved away to the Ol' Pasture since things were so unpleasant here because everybody said he screamed all night," continued Unc' Billy Possum. "He sat up all of one night just to make sho' that he didn't scream in his sleep, and he didn't make a sound the whole night long. The next mo'ning everybody said that he had been screaming just the same, and po' Sammy Jay just moved away. Yo' ought to be ashamed to play such jokes." Unc' Billy grinned as he said it.

"Thief! thief!" came in Sammy Jay's voice right out of the mouth of the owner of the long tail and sharp eyes. Then both little rascals laughed fit to kill themselves.

"Yo' come over to my house," said Unc' Billy. "My ol' woman sho' will be right smart glad to see yo', and she's gwine to be powerful surprised, deed she am! She done been laughing at me fo' a week, because Ah was sho' Ah done hear yo' that day."

So off the two started to see old Mrs. Possum, and for the rest of that night Sticky-toes the Tree Toad listened in vain for the sound of his own voice when his lips were closed tight.

XVIII
The Mischief-Makers

THERE was a dreadful time on the Green Meadows and in the Green Forest. Oh, dear, dear, dear! It really was dreadful! First Sammy Jay had been accused of screaming in the night and keeping honest little meadow and forest people awake when they wanted to sleep. And all the time Sammy Jay hadn't made a sound. Then Sticky-toes the Tree Toad had been accused of being noisy, when all the time he was sitting with his mouth closed as tight as tight could be.

All this was bad enough, but now things were so much worse that it was getting so that no one would have anything to do with any one else. Those who had been the very best of friends would pass without speaking. You see, everybody on the Green Meadows and in the Green Forest knows everybody else by their voice. So when Jimmy Skunk, happening along near the Smiling Pool, heard Mrs. Redwing's voice, he didn't waste any time trying to see Mrs. Redwing. Instead, he went straight over and told Johnny Chuck the unkind things that he had overheard Mrs. Redwing saying about Johnny.

In the same way Bobby Coon heard the voice of Blacky the Crow in Farmer Brown's corn-field, and

51

when Bobby listened, he heard some things not at all nice about himself. And so it was, all over the Green Meadows and through the Green Forest. It seemed as if almost everybody was heard talking about some one else, and never saying nice things. The only one who still managed to keep on good terms with everybody was Unc' Billy Possum. No one had ever heard him saying unkind things about others and so, because now there were so few others to talk to, everybody was glad to see Unc' Billy coming, and he soon was the best liked of all the little meadow and forest people. He went about trying to smooth out the troubles, and to see him you never, never would have guessed that he had anything to do with making them. My, my, no, indeed!

But every night when the moon was up, Unc' Billy would have a caller, who would come and sit just outside the doorway of Unc' Billy's house and scream "Thief! thief! thief!" Then out would pop Unc' Billy's sharp little face, and then his fat little body would follow, and he and his friend with the long tail and the sharp eyes, for of course you have guessed that is who it was, would put their heads together and laugh and chuckle as if they were enjoying the best joke ever was. Then they would whisper and sometimes talk right out loud, when they felt sure that no one was near to hear.

What were they talking about? Why, about the trouble on the Green Meadows and in the Green Forest, and what a joke it all was, and what was the best way to keep it up. You see, the reason that no one heard Unc' Billy saying mean things or heard any mean things said about Unc' Billy was because it was Unc' Billy himself and his friend with the long tail and the sharp eyes who were making all the trouble. Yes, Sir, they were the mischief-makers. It was great fun to fool everybody so. They never once stopped to think how very, very uncomfortable it kept everybody feeling.

XIX
Bobby Coon Makes a Discovery

BOBBY COON had overslept. Usually Bobby is astir shortly after jolly, round, red Mr. Sun has gone to bed behind the Purple Hills. But Bobby is very irregular in his habits. He is very fond of traveling about in the night, is Bobby Coon, and when he does that, he sleeps the greater part of the day. But once in a while he takes a notion to travel about by daylight, and when he does that, why of course he has to sleep part of the night, anyway. Bobby Coon is a very lucky chap, very lucky indeed, for he can see in the dark, and yet, unlike Hooty the Owl, he has no trouble in seeing in the broad daylight as well.

This night Bobby Coon had overslept because he had not gone to bed until the middle of the day. He had been prowling about and getting into mischief all of the night before and had not started for home until jolly, round Mr. Sun was smiling down from right overhead. By this time Bobby Coon had sticks in his eyes. He was so sleepy that it seemed to him that he never, never could get home. He was stumbling along through the Green Forest when he came to a hollow log. What do you think he did? Why, he crawled in there, and in two minutes was fast asleep, just as comfortable as if he had been in his own hollow tree.

There Bobby slept all the rest of the day and until long after Mr. Sun had pulled on his rosy nightcap. Perhaps he would have slept there all night, if he hadn't been waked up. It was the cry of "Thief! thief! thief!" that waked him. It seemed to come from right over his head.

"Sammy Jay ought to be ashamed of himself, waking honest people like this!" muttered Bobby Coon, as he yawned and stretched. At first he couldn't think where he was. Then he remembered. He was just getting ready to crawl out of the hollow log, when he heard something which made him stop and try to sit up so suddenly that he bumped his head. What he heard was the voice of Unc' Billy Possum, and he knew by the sound that Unc' Billy was sitting on the very log in which he himself was hiding.

"This is the greatest joke that ever was!" said Unc' Billy. "Pretty soon nobody on the Green Meadows or in the Green Forest will speak to anybody else excepting me. Yo' cert'nly have got all your ol' tricks with yo'."

"Yes," replied a voice which Bobby Coon had never heard before, but which he knew right away must belong to some one who had come from way down South where Unc' Billy Possum and Ol' Mistah Buzzard had come from. "Yes," said the voice, "Ah done got all mah ol' tricks and some more. But it's easy, Unc' Billy, it's easy to fool your new friends, because Ah reckon they never have been fooled this way before. Don' yo' think it is most time to stop? Ah don't want to show mahself in daylight. Besides, if Ah'm found out, nobody ain't gwine to have anything to do with me."

"Don't yo' worry. Nobody's gwine to find yo' out. We'll keep it up just a day or two longer. Yo' cert'nly am powerful good at imitating other people's voices. Ah wonder that Ol' Mistah Buzzard hasn't got his eye on yo' before now," said Unc' Billy Possum.

Bobby Coon had become wide awake as he listened. He tried hard to get a peep at the stranger with Unc' Billy, but all he could see was a long tail of feathers. Bobby waited until Unc' Billy and his friend had left. Then he crawled out of the hollow log, and he was chuckling to himself.

"I'll just have a little talk with Ol' Mistah Buzzard," said Bobby to himself.

XX
Bobby Coon and Ol' Mistah Buzzard
Have a Talk

BOBBY COON had spent the largest part of the forenoon sitting at the foot of the tall dead tree on which Ol' Mistah Buzzard likes to roost. All the time Ol' Mistah Buzzard had been sailing 'round and 'round in circles way up in the blue, blue sky, sometimes so high that to Bobby he looked like just a tiny speck. Bobby had watched him until his own neck ached. Mistah Buzzard hardly ever moved his wings. He just sailed and sailed and sailed up and down and 'round and 'round, just as if it was no work at all but pure fun, as indeed it was.

Bobby Coon had waited so long that it was almost more than he could do to be patient any longer, but if you really want a thing, it is worth waiting for, and so Bobby gave a great sigh and tried to make himself more comfortable. At last Mistah Buzzard came sailing down straight for the tall dead tree. With two or three flaps of his great wings he settled down on his favorite perch and looked down at Bobby Coon.

"Good mo'ning, Brer Coon," said Ol' Mistah Buzzard.

"Good mo'ning, Brer Coon," said Ol' Mistah Buzzard. *Page 57.*

"Good morning, Mistah Buzzard; I hope you are feeling very well this morning," replied Bobby Coon as politely as he knew how.

"Fair to middling well," said Ol' Mistah Buzzard, with a twinkle in his eyes. "What can Ah do fo' yo'all?"

"If you please, Mistah Buzzard, you can tell me if there is anybody way down South where you come from who can make his voice sound just like the voices of other people. Is there?" Bobby was using his very politest manner.

"Cert'nly! Cert'nly!" chuckled Ol' Mistah Buzzard. "It's Mistah Mockah the Mocking-bird. Why, that bird just likes to go around making trouble; he just naturally likes to. He just goes around mocking everything and everybody he hears, until sometimes it seems like yo' couldn't be sure of yo' own voice when yo' hear it. Why do yo' ask, Brer Coon?"

"Because he is right here in the Green Forest now," replied Bobby Coon.

"What's that yo' am a-saying, Brer Coon? What's that?" cried Ol' Mistah Buzzard, growing very excited.

Then Bobby Coon told Ol' Mistah Buzzard all about the trouble on the Green Meadows and in the Green Forest; how Sammy Jay had moved away to the Old Pasture so that no one could say that he screamed in the night, and yet how his voice was still heard; how Sticky-toes the Tree Toad was almost crazy because his neighbors said he was noisy, when all the time he was sitting with his mouth tight closed; and finally, how all the little meadow and forest people refused to speak to one another because of the many unkind things which had been overheard. And Bobby told what he had overheard the night before when Unc' Billy Possum and a stranger had sat on the very log in which Bobby had been taking a nap. Ol' Mistah Buzzard chuckled.

"Yo' might have known Unc' Billy was behind all that trouble," said he. "Yes, Sah, yo' might have known that ol' rascal was behind it. When Unc' Billy Possum and Mockah get their haids together, there sho'ly is gwine to be something doing."

XXI
Bobby Coon Has a Busy Day

BOBBY COON had left Ol' Mistah Buzzard sitting on his favorite dead tree. Every few minutes Ol' Mistah Buzzard would chuckle. "Brer Coon is right smart, and Ah reckon Unc' Billy Possum is gwine to get a taste of his own medicine. Yes, Sah, Ah reckon he is!" said Ol' Mistah Buzzard. Then he chuckled and chuckled, as he spread his broad wings and said: "Ah reckon Ah better be up in the blue, blue sky where Ah can look right down and see all the fun."

In the meantime Bobby Coon was hurrying back and forth across the Green Meadows and through the Green Forest, calling on all the little people who live there. He whispered a few words in the ear of one and then hurried on to whisper to the next one. When Bobby would first begin to whisper, the one to whom he was whispering would shake his head and look as if he didn't believe a word of what Bobby was saying. Then Bobby would point to Ol' Mistah Buzzard sailing 'round and 'round high up in the blue, blue sky where everybody could see him, and whisper some more. When he got through, he always carried away with him a promise that just what he had asked should be done.

Bobby Coon had thought of a plan to turn the joke on Unc' Billy Possum, and this was why he was hurrying back and forth whispering in the ears of every one who lived on the Green Meadows and in the Green Forest; that is everybody excepting Unc' Billy Possum and his family. It was the busiest day that Bobby Coon could remember.

It was the very next morning that Unc' Billy Possum was trotting along the Crooked Little Path down the hill. He was just starting out on his daily round of calls, and he was grinning as only Unc' Billy Possum can grin.

"Mah name is Billy Possum and mah home's a hollow
       tree!
By day or night Ah wander forth—it's all the same to
       me!
Ah fill mah stomach with an egg, or sometimes it is fish;
In fact Ah always helps mahself to anything Ah wish.
Fo' mah name is Billy Possum and mah other name is
       Smart;
To catch yo' Uncle Billy yo' must make an early start."

Unc' Billy was singing this to himself as he trotted along the Crooked Little Path, and all the time he was thinking of the great joke that he and his old friend Mr. Mocker, from way down South, were playing on the little people of the Green Meadows and the Green Forest.

This morning he was on his way to call first on Johnny Chuck. Half-way down the hill he met Bobby

Coon. Unc' Billy stopped and held out one hand as he said "Good mo'ning, Brer Coon. How do yo'all do this fine mo'ning?"

Bobby Coon walked right past as if he didn't see Unc' Billy at all. He didn't even look at him.

"What's the matter with yo' this mo'ning, Brer Coon?" shouted Unc' Billy. Bobby Coon kept right on, without so much as turning his head. Unc' Billy watched him, and there was a puzzled look on Unc' Billy's face. "Must be that Brer Coon has something powerful impo'tant on his mind," muttered Unc' Billy, as he started on.

Pretty soon he met Jimmy Skunk who had always been one of Unc' Billy's best friends. Jimmy was looking under every stick and stone for beetles for his breakfast.

"Good mo'ning, Neighbor Skunk!" said Unc' Billy in his heartiest voice.

Jimmy Skunk, who never hurries, kept right on pulling over sticks and stones just as if he didn't see or hear Unc' Billy at all. In fact, when he pulled over one stone, he dropped it right on Unc' Billy's tail and didn't seem to hear Unc' Billy's "Ouch!" as he pulled his tail from under the stone. Jimmy just went right on about his business.

Unc' Billy sat down and scratched his head. His face had lost the cheerful grin with which he had started out. Pretty soon he started on, but every few minutes he would stop and scratch his head thoughtfully. He didn't know what to make of Bobby

Coon and Jimmy Skunk. He was so surprised that he hadn't known whether to be angry or not.

"Ah must find out what Brer Chuck knows about it," thought Unc' Billy, as he trotted on.

XXII
Unc' Billy Possum Sees Many Backs

UNC' BILLY POSSUM was very sober as he hurried down the Lone Little Path to Johnny Chuck's house. He was very sober indeed, and that is very unusual for Unc' Billy Possum. It was very plain to see that something was bothering him. Johnny Chuck was sitting on his doorstep when Unc' Billy Possum came in sight, trotting down the Lone Little Path. As soon as Johnny saw him, he turned his back squarely towards Unc' Billy and pretended to be very much interested in something way off in the other direction. Unc' Billy came to a stop about two feet behind Johnny Chuck.

"A-hem!" said Unc' Billy.

Johnny Chuck sat there without moving, just as if he hadn't heard.

"It's a fine mo'ning," said Unc' Billy in his pleasantest voice.

Instead of replying, Johnny Chuck suddenly kicked up his heels and disappeared inside his house. Unc' Billy scratched his head with one hand and then with the other, and all the time his face grew more and more puzzled-looking. After a while he started on. Pretty soon he came to where Danny Meadow Mouse was playing all by himself. He didn't know

There sat the three little scamps on the Big Rock. *Page 67.*

that Unc' Billy was about until Unc' Billy said: "Good mo'ning, Brer Meadow Mouse."

Now Danny had always been delighted to see Unc' Billy Possum and to have a chat with him whenever Unc' Billy would stop. But this morning no sooner did Danny hear Unc' Billy's voice than he turned his back to Unc' Billy. This was more than Unc' Billy could stand. He reached out to take Danny Meadow Mouse by the ear to turn him around, but somehow Danny must have guessed what Unc' Billy meant to do, for without a word he ducked out of sight under the long grass, and hunt as he would Unc' Billy couldn't find him.

So Unc' Billy Possum gave it up and went on down to the Smiling Pool. There Little Joe Otter and Billy Mink and Jerry Muskrat were at play. They saw Unc' Billy coming, and when he reached the bank of the Smiling Pool there sat the three little scamps on the Big Rock, but all he could see was their backs.

"Hello, yo'alls!" shouted Unc' Billy.

Splash! All three had dived into the Smiling Pool, and though Unc' Billy waited and waited, he didn't see one of them again. Even Grandfather Frog turned his back to him and seemed very deaf that morning, though Unc' Billy tried and tried to make him hear.

All day long, wherever he went, Unc' Billy saw only the backs of his friends, and none of them seemed to see him at all. So he went home to his hollow tree in the Green Forest early that day to try and study out what it all meant.

XXIII
Unc' Billy Possum Consults Ol' Mistah Buzzard

OL' MISTAH BUZZARD has very sharp eyes. Nobody has sharper eyes than he. Swinging 'round and 'round and 'round and 'round in great circles way up in the blue, blue sky, so high that sometimes he looks like nothing but a little speck, he looks down and sees everything going on in the Green Meadows and a great deal that goes on in the Green Forest. There is very little that Ol' Mistah Buzzard misses. So all the day that Unc' Billy Possum had been tramping over the Green Meadows and through the Green Forest and finding everybody's back turned to him, Ol' Mistah Buzzard had been watching and laughing fit to kill himself. You see he knew all about Bobby Coon's visit to all the little meadow and forest people, and how Bobby had whispered in the ear of each that Unc' Billy Possum was partly to blame for all the trouble they had had lately.

Ol' Mistah Buzzard watched Unc' Billy go home and sit down with his chin in his hands and study and study, just as if he had something on his mind. By and by Unc' Billy looked up in the sky where Ol' Mistah Buzzard was sailing 'round and 'round. Then Unc' Billy hopped up mighty spry.

"Ah reckon Unc' Billy 'lows he'll make me a visit," said Ol' Mistah Buzzard with a chuckle, as he slid down, down out of the sky to the tall dead tree in the Green Forest, which is his favorite roosting-place. He hadn't been there long when Unc' Billy Possum came shuffling along, just as if he was out walking for his health.

"Howdy, Mistah Buzzard! Ah cert'nly hopes yo'all feel right smart," said Unc' Billy.

Ol' Mistah Buzzard's eyes twinkled as he replied: "Ah feel right pert, Brer Possum, thank yo'. Ah hopes yo' feel the same. Yo' look like nothing ever bothers yo'."

Unc' Billy grinned, but at the same time he looked a little foolish as he said: "That's right, Mistah Buzzard, that's right! Nothing ever does bother me." And all the time he was wondering however he should ask for Ol' Mistah Buzzard's advice and not let him know that something really was bothering him a great deal.

"Ah watched yo' take a long walk this mo'ning, Brer Possum," said Ol' Mistah Buzzard.

"Did yo', indeed; yo' have keen eyes, Mistah Buzzard!" replied Unc' Billy.

"Ah saw yo' meet a lot of yo' friends. It's fine to have a lot of friends, isn't it, Brer Possum?" said Ol' Mistah Buzzard.

Unc' Billy looked at Ol' Mistah Buzzard sharply. He wondered if Mistah Buzzard had noticed that all those friends had turned their backs on Unc' Billy that morning, but Mistah Buzzard looked as sober and solemn as a judge. All at once Ol' Mistah Buzzard hopped up and turned around, so that all Unc' Billy could see of him was his back. Unc' Billy stared, and for a minute he couldn't find his tongue. Then he heard a noise that sounded very much like a chuckle. In a few minutes it was a laugh. Finally Unc' Billy began to laugh too.

"Yo' take mah advice and bring mah ol' friend Mockah out of his hiding-place and introduce him to the Green Meadows and the Green Forest," said Ol' Mistah Buzzard.

Unc' Billy shook his head doubtfully. He was afraid that they might not forgive the tricks that Mr. Mocker had played on them, and then of course he couldn't stay in the Green Forest. So Unc' Billy scratched his head and thought and thought of how he could get Mr. Mocker out of the trouble he had got him into. Finally he went home and told all his troubles to old Mrs. Possum and asked her advice, as he should have done in the first place.

"Serves yo'alls right! It cert'nly does serve yo'alls right!" grunted Mrs. Possum, who was so busy looking after her eight lively babies that she had little time for fooling.

"Ah know it. It cert'nly does," replied Unc' Billy meekly.

"Mischief always trots ahead of grim ol' Mistah
　　Trouble,
They look and act enough alike to be each other's
　　double.

Whoever fools with Mischief's gwine to wake some day
    or other
And find that Trouble's just the same as Mischief's own
    twin brother."

Unc' Billy Possum listened to this just as if he had never heard it before, and nodded his head as if he agreed with every word of it. Old Mrs. Possum grumbled and scolded, but all the time she was thinking, and Unc' Billy knew that she was. Finally she finished sweeping the doorsteps and looked thoughtfully at Unc' Billy.

"Why don't yo' give a party fo' Mistah Mockingbird?" she inquired.

"The very thing!" cried Unc' Billy, and like a flash back came his old-time grin.

XXIV
Unc' Billy Possum Gives a Party

UNC' BILLY POSSUM'S party was the greatest event in the Green Forest since the famous surprise party which Peter Rabbit gave when Unc' Billy's family arrived from way down in Ol' Virginny. At first Unc' Billy had been afraid that no one would come. You see, he had been the cause of a lot of the trouble on the Green Meadows and in the Green Forest, and he knew that now all the little meadow and forest people had found him out. So he didn't dare send his invitations around by the Merry Little Breezes of Old Mother West Wind, for fear that no one would pay any heed to them. Of course that meant that Unc' Billy must take them around himself.

My, but that was hard work! It was the hardest work that Unc' Billy had ever done in all his life, for you know Unc' Billy is happy-go-lucky and takes things easy. But getting those invitations around— well, as Unc' Billy said, he "like to wore holes plumb through the soles of mah feet" before he got all of them delivered. It took him two whole days. In the first place there were so many to see. And then it was such hard work to deliver the invitations, because when his old friends saw him, they would promptly turn their backs to him and pretend they

72

didn't see him at all. Then Unc' Billy would take off his hat and make a sweeping bow just as if the one he was talking to was facing instead of back to him, and he would say:

> "Ah begs yo' pardon, 'deed Ah do,
> Fo' all the trouble Ah've caused yo',
> And hopes that Ah may sho'ly choke
> If it was meant fo' more'n a joke.
> So please fo'give ol' Uncle Bill
> And show yo' friendship for him still
> By taking this as an invite
> To join with me next Monday night
> Aroun' mah famous hollow tree,
> And help me to full merry be,
> And also meet a friend of mine;
> Ah'm sho' yo's bound to like him fine."

Then Unc' Billy would make another low bow and hurry on to the next one. Of course he couldn't tell whether or not any one would accept the invitation, but he went right on with his plans, just as if he expected everybody to be there. And when the time came, sure enough everybody was there, even Sammy Jay, to whom Unc' Billy had sent a special invitation by Ol' Mistah Buzzard. Mistah Buzzard had found Sammy Jay in the far-away Old Pasture, and Sammy had moved back to the Green Forest that very day.

Such a good time as everybody did have! There were heaps and heaps of good things to eat. They danced and played hide and seek. Finally Unc' Billy climbed up on a stump. He was dressed in his finest suit, and he wore his broadest grin. Everybody crowded around to hear what Unc' Billy was about to say.

"Mah friends and neighbors," said Unc' Billy, "Ah have a great surprise fo' yo'alls."

Then he stepped down, and everybody began to wonder and to guess what the surprise could be.

XXV
Unc' Billy Possum's Surprise

EVERYBODY was asking everybody else what the surprise could be which Unc' Billy had said he had for them. After he had made his speech, he had scurried out of sight, and no one could find him. Just about that time Billy Mink remembered that the party had been given to meet a friend of Unc' Billy Possum, but no friend had appeared.

Billy Mink spoke of the matter to Little Joe Otter, and Little Joe Otter spoke of the matter to Jerry Muskrat, and Jerry Muskrat spoke of the matter to Sammy Jay, and right while he was speaking there came a shrill scream of "Thief! thief! thief!" from a thick hemlock-tree near by, and the voice was just like the voice of Sammy Jay.

Sammy Jay became greatly excited. "There!" he cried. "You heard that when you was standing right in front of me and talking to me, Jerry Muskrat. You know that I wasn't making a sound! I told you that I hadn't been screaming in the night, and this proves it!"

Jerry Muskrat looked as if he couldn't believe his own ears. Just then the voice of Sticky-toes the Tree Toad began to croak "It's going to rain! It's going to rain! It's going to rain!" The voice seemed to come out of that very same hemlock-tree. Everybody noticed it and looked up at the tree, and while they were all trying to see Sticky-toes, something dropped plop right into their midst. It was Sticky-toes himself, and he had dropped from another tree altogether.

"You hear it!" he shrieked, dancing up and down he was so angry. "You hear it! It isn't me, is it? That's my voice, yet it isn't mine, because I'm right here! How can I be here and over there too? Tell me that!"

No one could tell him, and Sticky-toes continued to scold and sputter and swell himself up with anger. But everybody forgot Sticky-toes when they heard the voice of Blacky the Crow calling "Caw, caw, caw!" from the very same hemlock-tree. Now no one knew that Blacky the Crow had come to the party, for Blacky never goes abroad at night.

"Come out, Blacky!" they all shouted. But no Blacky appeared. Instead out of that magic hemlock-tree poured a beautiful song, so beautiful that when it ended everybody clapped their hands. After that there was a perfect flood of music, as if all the singers of the Green Forest and the Green Meadows were in that hemlock-tree. There was the song of Mr. Redwing and the song of Jenny Wren, and the sweet notes of Carol the Meadowlark and the beautiful happy song of Little Friend the Song Sparrow. No one had ever heard anything like it, and when it ended every one shouted for more. Even Sticky-toes the Tree Toad forgot his ill temper.

Instead of more music, out from the hemlock-tree flew a stranger. He was about the size of Sammy Jay and wore a modest gray suit with white trimmings. He flew over to a tall stump in the moonlight, and no sooner had he alighted than up beside him scrambled Unc' Billy Possum. Unc' Billy wore his broadest grin.

"Mah friends of the Green Forest and the Green Meadows, Ah wants yo'alls to know mah friend, Mistah Mocking-bird, who has come up from mah ol' home way down in 'Ol' Virginny.' He has the most wonderful voice in all the world, and when he wants to, he can make it sound just like the voice of any one of yo'alls. We uns is right sorry fo' the trouble we uns have made. It was all a joke, and now we asks yo' pardon. Mah friend Mistah Mockah would like to stay here and live, if yo'alls is willing," said Unc' Billy.

XXVI
Mr. Mocker Makes Himself at Home

AT first, when the little meadow and forest people were asked to pardon the tricks that Mr. Mocker and Unc' Billy Possum had played, a few were inclined not to. While they were talking the matter over, Mr. Mocker began to sing again that wonderful song of his. It was so beautiful that by the time it was ended, every one was ready to grant the pardon. They crowded around him, and because he is good-natured, he made his voice sound just like the voice of each one who spoke to him. Of course they thought that was great fun, and by the time Unc' Billy Possum's moonlight party broke up, Mr. Mocker knew that he had made so many friends that he could stay in the Green Forest as long as he pleased.

But there were a lot of little people who were not at Unc' Billy Possum's party, because they go to bed instead of going out nights. Of course they heard all about the party the next morning and were very anxious indeed to see the stranger with the wonderful voice. So Mr. Mocker went calling with Ol' Mistah Buzzard, and they visited all the little meadow and forest people who had not been at the party. Of course Mr. Mocker had to show off his wonderful

Sometimes he woke up in the night and
would sing for very joy. *Page 80*.

voice to each one. When he had finished, he was tuckered out, was Mr. Mocker, but he was happy, for now he had made friends and could live on the edge of the Green Forest with his old friends, Unc' Billy Possum and Ol' Mistah Buzzard.

So he soon made himself at home and, because he was happy, he would sing all day long. And sometimes, when the moon was shining, he woke up in the night and would sing for very joy. Now Peter Rabbit thought the newcomer's voice such a wonderful thing that he used to follow him around just to hear him fool others by making his voice sound like theirs. It was great fun. Peter and Mocker became great friends, and so when Peter heard it whispered around that Mr. Mocking-bird had not come by his wonderful voice honestly, he didn't believe a word of it and was very indignant. Of course he couldn't go to Mr. Mocker himself and ask him, for he didn't want Mr. Mocker to know that such unkind things were being said. Finally he thought of Grandfather Frog, who is very old and very wise. "He'll know," said Peter, as off he posted to the Smiling Pool.

"If you please, Grandfather Frog, how does it happen that Mr. Mocker has such a wonderful voice and can make it sound like the voice of any one whom he hears?" asked Peter.

Now Grandfather Frog was feeling out of sorts that morning. He hadn't heard the whisper that Mr. Mocker had not come by his voice honestly, and he thought that Peter Rabbit was asking just to hear a story.

"Chugarum!" replied Grandfather Frog crossly. "Go ask Mr. Buzzard." And that was all that Peter could get out of him. So, not knowing what else to do, off started Peter Rabbit to ask Ol' Mistah Buzzard where his friend Mr. Mocking-bird got such a wonderful voice.

Ol' Mistah Buzzard laughed when he heard that some folks said that Mr. Mocker had not come by his voice honestly.

"There isn't a word of truth in it, Brer Rabbit," he declared. "Yo' go tell all your friends that Mistah Mockah is the best loved of all the birds way down Souf."

And this is all for the present about the adventures of Mr. Mocker the Mocking-bird. But others have had adventures, and one is Jerry Muskrat. The next book will tell all about them.

THE END